Would You Like A Scarlet Striped Schrinkler?

Virginia K. White

By Virginia K. White
Illustrated by Gaspar Sabater

This book belongs to:

This is a
Scarlet Striped
Schrinkler!

It loves snazzy shocks of hair,
Sometimes styled
So swirly and snappy.

It lives in schools, shadows, shoes, sheds, and sacks.

A Scarlet Striped Schrinkler eats Spinach, Sandwiches, Soup, and Salads.

Sometimes it even eats shellfish, seaweed, snappers, and sushi.

A Scarlet Striped Schrinkler never eats snakes!

It likes skiing, sleeping, snowboarding, and smooching.

Sometimes it even
likes swimming, sailing,
swinging, and sliding.

A Scarlet Striped Schrinkler never likes seesawing!

It wants to be a Songwriter,
Soprano Singer,
Scholar, or Sculptor.

Sometimes it even wants to be
a Spy, Signmaker, or
a Sassy Serenader.

A Scarlet Striped Schrinkler
never wants to be
a Starry-eyed Stagehand.

It slithers, scampers, scuffles, and scurries.

Sometimes it even likes to scowl, sneer, shout, or scream.

A Scarlet Striped Schrinkler
never shoves!

One day, a Scarlet Striped Schrinkler slipped onto my sweater. It squeaked, squealed, and scratched my shoulder.

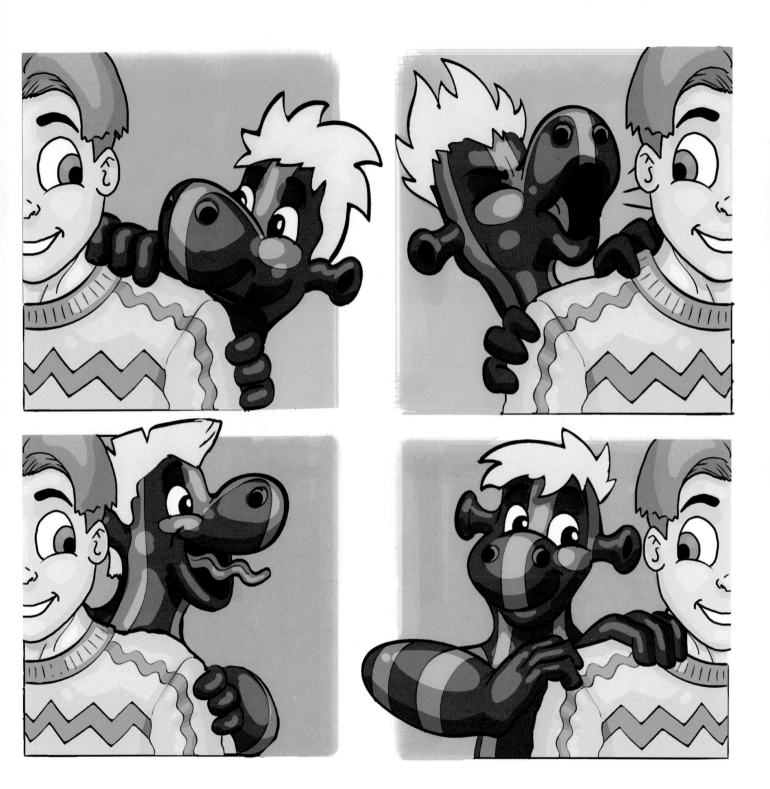

I Swiftly Silenced the Scarlet Striped Schrinkler by Serenading it and Saying I would Stir up a Saucy Seaweed Stew complete with Squash and Sprinkles.

The Scarlet Striped Schrinkler Said I was a Sweetheart. After Snacking, we Sat in the Summer Sunshine and Snuggled.

Would you like to have a Scarlet Striped Schrinkler visit you?

Virginia K. White is a retired English teacher and author of the *Little Honker Series* and *Glasses for Margie*. Kids and animals have always been a huge part of her life. While searching for an interesting way to teach alliteration to her students, she created a short version of the Scarlet Striped Schrinkler for her Creative Writing students and later expanded the adventures into *Would You Like a Scarlet Striped Schrinkler?*

Gaspar D. Sabater graduated from the visual art school in Mar del Plata as a professional illustrator. He also studied with artists in the comic and graphic industry which provided him an opportunity to reach and develop children's imagination and creativity through art. While working as a penciler for a comic publishing house, he realized his passion was communicating with kids in the creative language of art. He is the illustrator for Virginia's *Little Honker Series* and *Glasses for Margie*.

Made in the USA
Columbia, SC
17 November 2019